Mozart's Banana

Mozart's Banana

Gillian Cross

With illustrations by
Richard Morgan

Barrington Stoke

To the wonderful
Sturminster Newton mobile library

First published in 2014 in Great Britain by
Barrington Stoke Ltd
18 Walker Street, Edinburgh, EH3 7LP

www.barringtonstoke.co.uk

This story was first published in a different form in
Stacks of Stories (Hodder Children's books, 1997)

A CIP catalogue record for this book is available
from the British Library upon request

ISBN: 978-1-78112-367-6

Printed in China by Leo

Contents

1   A Crazy Horse   1

2   Sammy's Kingdom   8

3   Understand Your Horse   14

4   A Saddle and a Bridle   19

5   The Madness   25

6   Swan Lake   42

Chapter 1
A Crazy Horse

He was called Mozart's Banana – a crazy name
for a crazy horse.

Most of the time, he had the sweetest
temper in the world. You could rub his nose
and pull his ears and he was as gentle as
a kitten. But try to get on his back, and –
POWAKAZOOM!

He went mad. He bucked. He reared. He bolted round the field and scraped himself against every tree.

Of course, at first we all tried to tame him.

Every child in the village had a go – until Sammy Foster tore his arm on the barbed wire. Then our mothers all marched up to see old Mrs Clausen, who owned the horse. Mrs Clausen said, "NO MORE." She said that if we went into the field again she'd call the police.

After that, no one bothered with Mozart's Banana. Not until Alice Brett came.

Alice Brett had never been near a horse in her life. She was a skinny little thing with wispy hair and big eyes, like a Yorkshire terrier, and she had lived in the middle of

a town until then. She looked as if she'd be scared stiff of anything bigger than a hamster, let alone a horse like Mozart's Banana.

Sammy Foster warned Alice about Mozart's Banana, the way he warned all the new kids. On her first day at school, he pulled up his sleeve and waved his arm in her face.

"See that?" he said. "What d'you think did that?"

Sammy had a fantastic scar from the barbed wire. It was long and ragged and dark purple. Most kids pulled faces and edged away when they saw it, but Alice Brett hardly gave it a glance.

"Been fighting?" she said.

"Fighting?" Sammy pushed the scar right under her nose. "How would anyone get *that* in a fight, Mouse Brain? 69 stitches, I needed."

Alice Brett looked at him with pity, as if he hadn't got a clue. Sammy went red in the face and grabbed her by the collar.

"You think that's nothing?" he said. "Well, you try and ride that flaming horse, if you're so tough. I bet you £10 you break your neck."

He gave her a shake and stamped off.

Alice pulled her collar straight, as cool as a choc-ice. That evening she was up at the Church Field, staring over the gate.

Chapter 2
Sammy's Kingdom

That was how it began.

For weeks and weeks, Alice leaned on that gate and stared at Mozart's Banana as he trotted round the field. Every now and then, he stopped and stared back at her with his great, melting eyes. That was all. But she didn't miss a day, rain or shine.

"What are you trying to do?" Sammy said. "Cast a spell on him?"

Alice kept her mouth shut and smiled a little, silent smile that drove Sammy mad.

Then she started coming to the library.

That annoyed Sammy, too. He was a favourite with Mrs Grant, who drove the library van. Every Thursday, Mrs Grant gave him a special smile as she checked out his books.

"Hope you enjoy them," she would say. "Let me know what you think next week."

The library was part of Sammy's kingdom, like the school playground and the park. He was always first out of school on Thursday afternoons, and first up to the War Memorial, where the library van was parked. No one

dared check out a book until he'd looked at it,
in case he wanted to read it.

Until Alice came.

Alice didn't race out of school to be there
first. And she didn't scrabble about on the
shelves with the rest of us. She walked up on

her own, whispered something to Mrs Grant and filled in a little white card. Then she went up on the hill, to see Mozart's Banana.

That was the first week.

The second week, Alice came back and whispered again, and Mrs Grant felt under the counter and fetched her out a book.

"There you are," she said. "Hope you enjoy it." And she smiled. Her special smile.

Sammy dived out of the van and grabbed Alice's arm as she walked off. "What are you up to? Let's see that book," he demanded.

"It's mine," Alice said, in her thin, clear voice. "I ordered it. You leave go of me."

Mrs Grant stuck her head out of the van and said, "*Sammy!*" She looked really shocked. Alice pulled her arm free and ran away.

The third week, Alice had another book on order, but this time Sammy was more cunning.

He hung around until the van was gone and when Alice came back down from the Church Field he stuck out his foot and tripped her over. Alice hit the road with a thump and Sammy hooked her bag out of her hand and turned it upside down.

Chapter 3
Understand Your Horse

By the time Alice got to school the next day, everyone knew she was reading a book called *Understand Your Horse*.

We all told her no one could understand Mozart's Banana.

"If you can understand that horse," Sammy said, "I can dance *Swan Lake*." And he hopped round the playground on one leg like a ballet dancer.

Alice just listened with a polite smile and went off without answering.

Then Alice turned up at the riding school.

That was Sammy's kingdom, too. His big
sister worked there, and he fancied himself as
an expert – despite the fact he hadn't been on a
horse since he'd tried to ride Mozart's Banana.

When Alice started to spend Saturdays at
the stables, Sammy was furious.

"She's not paying," he said, to make sure
everyone knew. "They're giving her lessons for
free because she helps with mucking out."

Sammy tried to make a joke of it, by
holding his nose when Alice went past and
complaining about a smell in the classroom.
But that didn't bother Alice. She just went
on doing the same things. She ordered horse
books from the library on Thursdays. She
helped at the stables on Saturdays. And (of

course) she talked to Mozart's Banana every evening. Rain or shine.

But, even then, we never thought she'd try to get on his back.

She must have been planning it for weeks, ever since she heard about the fancy dress competition. Every year, in Book Week, we all dressed up as characters from stories, and old Mrs Clausen gave a prize for the best costume.

"Suppose *you're* coming as Black Beauty," Sammy said to Alice.

She gave him a long, interested stare. "Good idea. Thanks," she replied.

Chapter 4
A Saddle and a Bridle

Alice wasn't joking about Black Beauty being a good idea.

She spent three weeks working on her horse mask. And when it was finished, she took it up to show them at the riding stables.

Sammy heard all about that, of course.

"My sister said you looked really stupid," he told Alice. "After you'd gone, they all laughed at you."

If Alice minded, she didn't show it. She'd got what she wanted, after all. The riding school people had let her borrow a saddle and a bridle as part of her fancy dress.

On the Thursday of Book Week, Alice came into school wearing black leggings, a black jumper and the horse's head mask. She had the bridle over one arm and the saddle over the other.

Sammy thought Alice was going to win the prize and he was twice as nasty as usual. All morning he made snide comments and pulled her hair. Alice didn't take any notice. But, at the start of the afternoon, she went up to the teacher's desk.

"Please, Miss," she said. "I feel sick. Can I go home?"

"Oh, Alice! You'll miss the judging," Miss Bellamy said.

"I don't mind that. Honest, Miss. I just –"

Alice looked as if she might throw up any moment. Miss Bellamy rushed her off to the office to phone her parents, but there was no one in.

"You'll have to lie down in the staff room,"
Miss Bellamy said. "Have a little sleep, and
maybe you'll be all right for the competition."

"All right, Miss."

Alice sounded as meek as usual. But when
we went to fetch her at 3 p.m., she wasn't there.
There was just the horse's head, on the chairs
where she'd been lying. And a note.

"GONE HOME," it said.

By then, all the parents were there to see the fancy dress, and old Mrs Clausen was pulling up in her car.

No one had a moment to go and chase after Alice.

No one had time to wonder why she'd left the horse mask – and taken the saddle and bridle with her.

Chapter 5
The Madness

Sammy came top in the fancy dress. He always won things like that.

Mrs Clausen said he was the best Long John Silver she'd ever seen, and he got a badge and a book token for £10. Sammy went round and showed everyone, and he couldn't wait for school to finish.

"I'm going to take them to the library van!" he shouted. "And show Mrs Grant my fancy dress!"

The moment the bell rang, Sammy charged out of school. The library van was just pulling up by the War Memorial, and he threw himself into it, stuffed parrot and all.

"Look, Mrs Grant! I won!" he yelled.

"Well done!" Mrs Grant said. She gave him her special smile – the first one for weeks. "No need to ask who you're meant to be," she said. "You look wonderful! Just like –"

Then Mrs Grant heard the sound of clattering hooves. We all heard it. Mrs Grant looked past Sammy and her face went dead white.

Mozart's Banana was galloping down the road towards us at top speed, rolling his eyes and snorting. On his back, clutching his mane, was Alice Brett.

She'd done it all by herself. She'd sneaked up to Church Field with the saddle and bridle. She'd got them on to the horse while Mrs Clausen was out of the way at the fancy dress competition. She'd held him steady while she climbed on his back. And then –

That's when the madness always hits Mozart's Banana. The moment he feels someone in the saddle. He takes off straight away, galloping round the field, bucking and rearing.

None of us had ever lasted longer than half a minute.

But Alice had stuck on all the way round the field and clung on tight when Mozart's Banana headed down the hill, completely out of control.

"Everybody into the van!" Mrs Grant
screamed.

We all jumped in and shut the door – just in time. The horse went past like a thunder-bolt. If we hadn't moved, he would have charged over us.

"Alice is mad!" Sammy yelled. "She'll be killed!"

"Don't be so silly!" Mrs Grant snapped.

But Sammy was right and she knew it. We all knew it.

Mozart's Banana didn't turn at the bend, where the road went round the park. He jumped the hedge and carried straight on, like a cannon-ball. Alice was still on his back when he landed, but she wasn't in the saddle any more.

There were three more hedges before the railway line. A tunnel ran under the line and beyond that was the slip road to –

THE MOTORWAY!

We all saw the same picture in our minds. A crazy horse charging under the railway, across the slip road and out into six lanes of traffic. With Alice on his back.

"We've got to stop him!" Sammy shouted.

"Yes, we must!" Mrs Grant jumped into the driving seat. "Lie down, you lot! And hold on tight!"

Mrs Grant turned on the engine and threw the van into gear.

As we screeched away, round the War
Memorial and down the hill, we had a glimpse

of the school. All the other children had run out to see what was going on. Teachers were shouting and parents were waving their arms about. Mrs Grant didn't waste time on any of them. She stamped on the gas and roared down the hill.

As Mrs Grant swung the van round the first corner, books slithered onto our heads. We struggled to get free of them as she swung the van round the second corner, in the other direction. After that, we decided that lying down was too dangerous. We sat up and held on to the shelves, and cheered the library van on.

"Hurry, Miss! You've nearly caught them!" Ellen Jones shouted.

"He's got to jump another hedge!" yelled Ross Parks. "That'll slow him down!"

The road and the field ran side by side down the hill, for about half a mile. We could all see that the van was going to overtake the horse – but what could Mrs Grant do then?

As we drove under the railway bridge, Mrs Grant yelled back to us. "Get ready to jump out and open the bottom gate! But not till I say!"

I was still baffled, but Sammy had understood.

The moment the van stopped, Sammy yanked the door open and threw himself out. There was a narrow strip of field on our right, between the railway and the slip road. Sammy raced across to the field gate and heaved it open. As soon as it was wide enough, Mrs Grant swung the van round and we bumped across the field at top speed, with Sammy running behind.

The tunnel under the railway line was meant for cows and it was narrow and dark. Mrs Grant raced to block it, before Mozart's Banana could gallop inside. It should have worked. With any other horse, it would have

worked. The van was in front of the tunnel by the time we heard the sound of hooves. We all held our breath as the noise came closer, and we waited for the galloping to slow down. It had to slow down. That was the only sensible thing for the horse to do.

We should have known that Mozart's Banana was too crazy to be sensible. He didn't even break step. He just gathered himself together and –

"Oh, no!" Mrs Grant said. "I don't believe it! He's going to jump!"

There was no time to do anything. The horse launched himself off the ground in one beautiful movement. He soared higher than any horse I've ever seen, with Alice Brett clinging on to his neck.

He couldn't do it, of course. Not even
Mozart's Banana could make a jump like that.
It was impossible.

There was an enormous thud, and a horrible scrape of metal on metal as his horse-shoes scrabbled down the side of the van. And there was a soft slithering noise across the roof.

"Stay inside!" Mrs Grant snapped. "All of you!"

She pushed the door open and we all crowded in behind her, to see what had happened.

Mozart's Banana lay on the ground by the van with a dazed look on his face. There was no sign of Alice. She'd slid right across the roof and landed on the other side.

But Alice didn't stay there. While we were still gazing at the horse, she marched round the front of the van. She had mud on her face and her riding hat over one eye. She didn't take the least bit of notice of any of us. She marched straight up to Mozart's Banana.

"Well?" she scolded him. "Was that stupid or what?"

Mozart's Banana looked up at her with big, dizzy eyes and Alice grabbed his reins and

pulled. With one puzzled look, he scrambled to his feet and stood and hung his head while Alice told him off.

You don't want to know what she said. If I wrote it down, no one would let you read this story. Even Sammy looked shocked when he reached us.

"What did you say?" he asked.

Alice just pushed the reins at him. "Hold those," she commanded.

And Alice grabbed hold of the saddle and pulled herself up. No one tried to stop her, because no one dreamed, not for a minute, that she'd do anything so stupid.

"Alice!" Mrs Grant said. "You can't –"

"He'll be fine now," Alice said. "Come on, you lot. Walk us back to the field."

Chapter 6
Swan Lake

And that was how we went back to the field with Alice and Mozart's Banana.

The whole crowd of us went, in our fancy dress. Long John Silver, Mary Poppins, Little Red Riding Hood and two Charlie Buckets. And, in the middle of us, Mozart's Banana. He still looked dazed, and he plodded along like a

seaside donkey. And Alice sat on his back, with
mud on her nose and a great rip in the knee of
her leggings.

We went right past the parents and the teachers and old Mrs Clausen, all the way up to the Church Field. Sammy opened the gate and Alice rode in and slid off the horse's back. She held out her muddy, grazed hand.

"That's £10 you owe me, Sammy Foster," she said.

Sammy swallowed hard and stared at her. Then he put his hand into his pocket and pulled out the book token he'd just won. "This OK?" he asked.

Alice opened the book token, nodded and tucked it into her pocket. By that time, Mrs Clausen was roaring into the field.

"You stupid girl!" she yelled. "That's the most dangerous thing I've ever seen."

Alice gave her a long, sad look, as if she knew about things that were a lot more dangerous. "I won't do it again," she said.

"Mozart's Banana doesn't like it. He hates being pushed around."

Mrs Clausen stared back at her, with her mouth open. Then she nodded. "Fine. You can come into the field whenever you like," she said.

"Thanks," said Alice.

And she did. Alice went up every evening, sat on the gate and chatted to Mozart's Banana. But she never tried to get on his back again. He might be crazy, but Alice wasn't.

And the next time the library van came round, Mrs Grant reached under the counter as we all walked in. "Here you are, Sammy," she said.

Sammy blinked. "I never ordered anything."

"I think someone ordered it for you," Mrs Grant said.

Everyone crowded round to read the title of the book and we all started to laugh.

The book was called *Ballet for Beginners*.

"What on earth –?" Sammy said.

Alice smiled her little, silent smile. "Time to dance *Swan Lake*, Sammy Foster."

Our books are tested
for children and young people by
children and young people.

Thanks to everyone who consulted on
a manuscript for their time and effort in
helping us to make our books better
for our readers.

The Mystery of the Man with the Black Beard

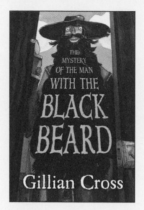

Pink sticky stuff on the ground

Extra-large boots hidden in the garden

A strange man in an orange van ...

Annie Clark's dad is the perfect guy to solve clues – he's a Crime Buster. But he's missing! First a visitor with a big black beard calls round – and then Bill Clark vanishes into thin air.

Now Annie and her friends must take their turn to follow the clues and find Annie's dad before it's too late ...

The Monster Snowman

Eyes from light bulbs

A nose from a broken bottle

Teeth from bits of glass ...

Jack, Ryan and Sam have built the biggest, scariest snowman ever. It's a Monster Snowman – and it even has a phone!

But later that night, Jack gets a weird text. It's not from Sam or Ryan. Who wants Jack to come out to play ...?

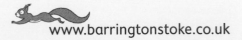

www.barringtonstoke.co.uk

More *4u2read* titles ...

All Sorts to Make a World
JOHN AGARD

Shona's day has been packed with characters. First there was 3.2-million-year-old Lucy in the Natural History Museum, and then Pinstripe Man, Kindle Woman, Doctor Bananas and the iPod Twins.

Now Shona and her dad are on a Tube train that's stuck in a tunnel and everyone around them is going ... bananas!

Nadine Dreams of Home
BERNARD ASHLEY

Nadine finds Britain real scary. Not scary like soldiers, or burning buildings, or the sound of guns. But scary in other ways. If only her father were here with Nadine, her mother and her little brother. They have no idea if they will ever see Nadine's father again.

But then Nadine finds a special picture, and dreams a special dream ...

Deadly Letter
MARY HOFFMAN

"Ip dip sky blue.
Who's it? Not you."

Prity wants to play with the other children at school, but it's hard when you're the new girl and you don't know the rules. And it doesn't help when you're saddled with a name that sounds like a joke. Will Prity ever fit in?

Gnomes, Gnomes, Gnomes
ANNE FINE

Sam's a bit obsessed. Any time he gets his hands on some clay, he makes gnomes. Dozens of them live out in the shed. But when Sam's mum needs that space, she says the gnomes will have to go. And so Sam plans a send-off for his little clay friends – a send-off that turns into a night the family will never forget!

www.barringtonstoke.co.uk